W.i.t.c.h.

Will Irma Taranee Cornelia Hay Lin

Part V.
The Book of Elements
Volume 1

W.i.t.c.h.

Will   Irma   Taranee   Cornelia   Hay Lin

Part V.
The Book of Elements
Volume 1

CONTENTS

Between Dream and Reality

"A true warrior knows when she needs help."

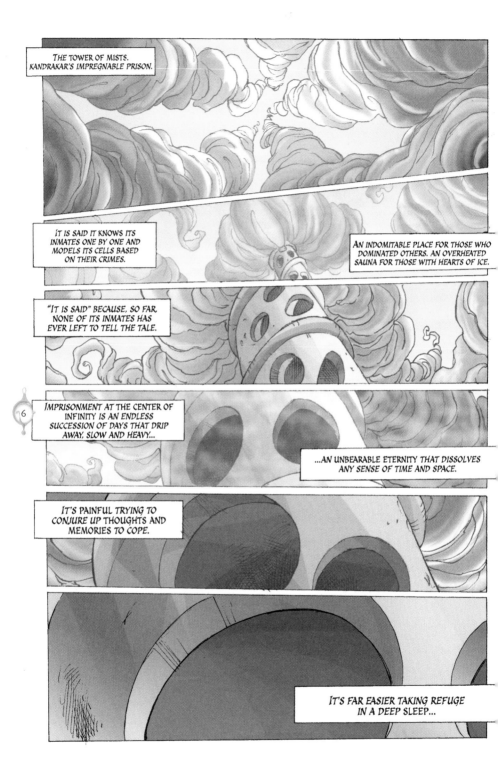

THE TOWER OF MISTS.
KANDRAKAR'S IMPREGNABLE PRISON.

IT IS SAID IT KNOWS ITS
INMATES ONE BY ONE AND
MODELS ITS CELLS BASED
ON THEIR CRIMES.

AN INDOMITABLE PLACE FOR THOSE WHO
DOMINATED OTHERS. AN OVERHEATED
SAUNA FOR THOSE WITH HEARTS OF ICE.

"IT IS SAID" BECAUSE, SO FAR,
NONE OF ITS INMATES HAS
EVER LEFT TO TELL THE TALE.

IMPRISONMENT AT THE CENTER OF
INFINITY IS AN ENDLESS
SUCCESSION OF DAYS THAT DRIP
AWAY, SLOW AND HEAVY...

...AN UNBEARABLE ETERNITY THAT DISSOLVES
ANY SENSE OF TIME AND SPACE.

IT'S PAINFUL TRYING TO
CONJURE UP THOUGHTS AND
MEMORIES TO COPE.

IT'S FAR EASIER TAKING REFUGE
IN A DEEP SLEEP...

THE KING OF LIES IS NO DIFFERENT. LOCKED IN A CELL OF PAINFUL ILLUSIONS, HE SEEKS COMFORT IN DREAMS—THE EXCEPTION PROVING THE RULE IN THE TOWER'S THOUSAND-YEAR HISTORY...

HE MANAGED TO ESCAPE... ONLY TO BE LOCKED UP AGAIN...

...AND NOW, HE DOESN'T KNOW WHAT FATE AWAITS HIM.

CEDRIC'S SLUMBER IS UNEASY...

...A CRUEL SLEEP THAT BRINGS BACK TO HIM THE TERRIBLE MOMENT WHEN HIS ESCAPE WAS THWARTED...

GET UP, CEDRIC... AND LISTEN CAREFULLY.

...I WONDER HOW *ORUBE'S* DOING!

PFFFT!

WHY? SHE TAKING PART IN A *CAT SHOW*?

YOU CLEARLY *DON'T REMEMBER* SHE ANSWERED AN AD IN THE *HEATHERFIELD NEWS*!

UH...NO! MUSTA DELETED THE INFO TO MAKE ROOM FOR THAT *SPAGHETTI CARBONARA RECIPE*!

BUT...YOU DO REMEMBER SHE *STARTED AT UNIVERSITY*, RIGHT?

INSIGNIFICANT DETAIL, SINCE SHE DIDN'T EVEN BOTHER TO INTRODUCE US TO HER NEW CLASS-MATES...

...ESPECIALLY THE *CUTE* ONES, OBVIOUSLY!

OKAY, OKAY! RECAP FOR THOSE WHO MISSED IT: ORUBE IS STUDYING *JOURNAL-ISM*...

...SO SHE'S BEEN CHECKING THE PAPERS FOR *JOBS*...

...BECAUSE SHE NEEDS MORE MONEY THAN SHE EARNS AT MR. OLSEN'S PET SHOP... ⸙CRUNCH⸙

CRON CH

WELL, IT'S JUST FOR A FEW HOURS A DAY...

BESIDES... MAYBE SHE WANTS TO HANG OUT WITH PEOPLE HER OWN AGE!

UM... CAN I FINISH?

15

YOU ROCK, TARANEE

33

COME IN. IT'S YOUR TURN!

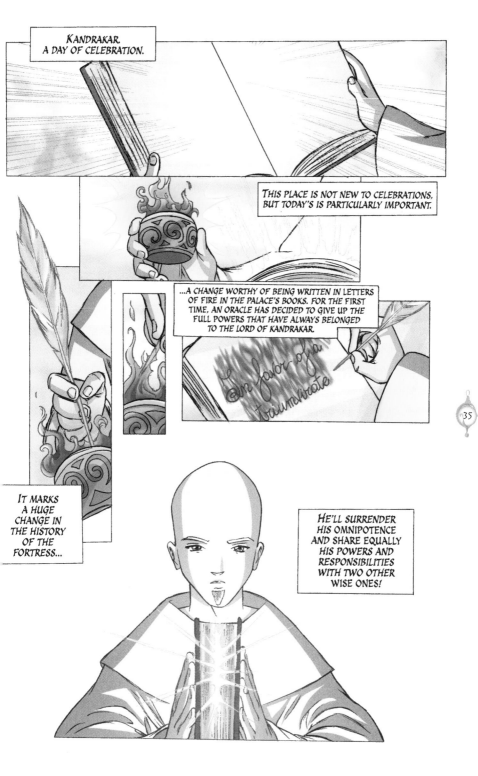

KANDRAKAR.
A DAY OF CELEBRATION.

THIS PLACE IS NOT NEW TO CELEBRATIONS,
BUT TODAY'S IS PARTICULARLY IMPORTANT.

...A CHANGE WORTHY OF BEING WRITTEN IN LETTERS
OF FIRE IN THE PALACE'S BOOKS. FOR THE FIRST
TIME, AN ORACLE HAS DECIDED TO GIVE UP THE
FULL POWERS THAT HAVE ALWAYS BELONGED
TO THE LORD OF KANDRAKAR.

IT MARKS
A HUGE
CHANGE IN
THE HISTORY
OF THE
FORTRESS...

HE'LL SURRENDER
HIS OMNIPOTENCE
AND SHARE EQUALLY
HIS POWERS AND
RESPONSIBILITIES
WITH TWO OTHER
WISE ONES!

SIR! HOW ARE YOU FEELING?

LIKE ONE WHO, FOR THE *FIRST TIME*, KNOWS HE IS *NOT ALONE* CARRYING A GREAT BURDEN...

...*RELIEVED AND HOPEFUL*. THAT IS HOW I FEEL, SISTER YAN LIN!

THANK YOU FOR BEING WILLING TO *SHARE* THIS *WEIGHT* WITH ME...

...AND THANK YOU ALL, WISE ONES, FOR HAVING ACCEPTED MY DECISION!

IF, IN *THE EYES OF THE WORLD, THE DIVISION* OF POWER MAY SEEM WEAK...

HE JUST KEEPS TALKING...

...IN THE *EYES OF THE SPIRIT*, IT APPEARS AS *STRENGTH*!

OUCH!

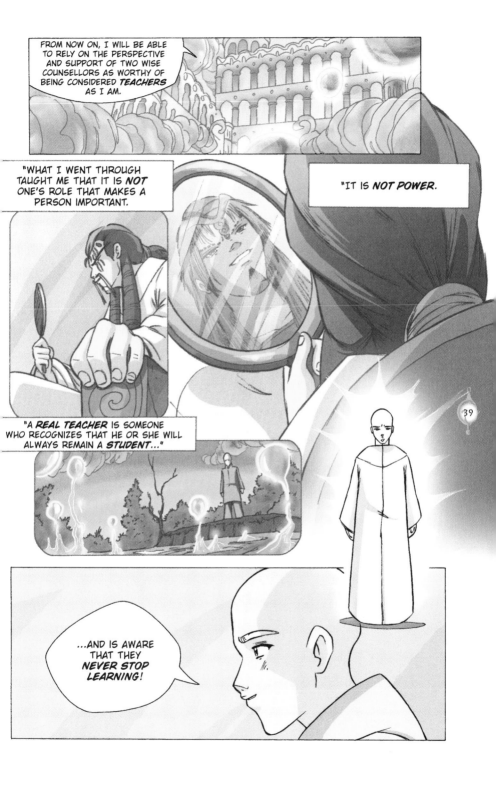

53

58

ERIC...I'M SORRY... I DIDN'T MEAN...

IT'S OKAY. IT'S NOT YOU. IT'S JUST...THAT'S THE POINT...

...THE *SECOND THING*, I MEAN...

IT'S THAT THIS TIME, MOM AND DAD...

...HAVE ASKED ME TO *GO WITH THEM*...

END OF CHAPTER

Will   Irma   Taranee   Cornelia   Hay Lin

FIRE...

...AIR...

...WATER...

...EARTH...

...AND WILL'S PURE ENERGY.

67

HEY, WE'VE BEEN HERE BEFORE!

YES. IT WAS YAN LIN WHO SHOWED YOU THIS MAGICAL SPOT.*

*IT'S THE ROOM OF PHANTOMS. SEE W.I.T.C.H. CHAPTER 47

THIS IS WHERE ALL THE *IMMATERIAL COPIES* OF MAGICAL OBJECTS ARE KEPT.

INCLUDING THE HOUR-GLASS OF THE BREATH OF TIME! YOU REMEMBER IT, DO YOU NOT, CORNELIA?

HOW COULD I FORGET? PHOBOS GAVE IT TO ME. IT WAS A TRICK!

YET, IT GLADLY ACCEPTED YOU. JUST LOOK! IT SHINES WITH JOY.

IT RECOGNIZES ME? FOR REAL?

YES. BUT IT IS NOT YET TIME FOR YOU TO BE REUNITED.

"...TO THE RAINY DAY WHEN WILL ARRIVED IN HEATHER-FIELD!*

*SEE W.I.T.C.H. #1

"BACK THEN, SHE COULD NOT HAVE KNOWN THAT EVIL FORCES WERE WAITING, PREPARED TO ELIMINATE HER!

"SO WILL MET HER NEW FRIENDS, WITH WHOM SHE FORGED A SPECIAL BOND.

"BUT WHAT INTERESTS US IS A CRUCIAL MOMENT THAT TOOK PLACE AT HAY LIN'S HOUSE.

YOU, IRMA, WILL HAVE POWER OVER *WATER*, UNBROKEN AND UNCONTAINABLE...

"THAT IS... THE MOMENT WISE YAN LIN SHOWED YOU FUTURE GUARDIANS ...

"...A WONDER-FUL REALITY, THOUGH DIFFICULT TO ACCEPT!"

SO WE...I MEAN... *THEY* WOULDA SPLIT UP 'COS OF ME! WHY DO I FREEZE THIS WAY?

EVEN WHEN WE ARE INDECISIVE, SOMEHOW WE MAKE DECISIONS.

BUT HERE COMES *ELYON.* SHE HAS BEEN *BRAIN-WASHED* INTO LURING YOU INTO A *TRAP...*

...IN THE SCHOOL *GYM!* THAT'S WHAT HAPPENED IN OUR PAST!

BUT IN *THIS* PAST, IRMA AND HAY LIN DON'T FEEL LIKE FOLLOWING HER, SO...

...*EVIL* WILL HAVE TO TEMPORARILY GIVE UP ON ITS PLANS.

SO ALL'S WELL THAT ENDS WELL.

81

LET US NOT JUMP TO CONCLUSIONS. KEEP WATCHING!

"WATCH THE REAL CONSEQUENCES OF THIS DECISIVE... INDECISION!"

SHE STARTED IT!

82

THINK ABOUT IT. TARANEE, TOUCH. ME, SIGHT. IRMA, TASTE...

...CORNELIA, SMELL. AND HAY LIN...HEARING!

THE FIVE SENSES!

YES, FIVE! LIKE US. OR LIKE A SINGLE PERSON!

AFTER A CHAT WITH MY MOM...THAT'S WHEN I UNDERSTOOD AND DECIDED TO RISK IT.

YES. FROM NOW ON, I'M LEAVING FEAR TO SOMEONE WHO ISN'T LUCKY ENOUGH TO HAVE FRIENDS...

...LIKE

YOU!

95

SO THE HEART OF KANDRAKAR APPEARED A SECOND TIME, GIVING YOU BACK...

...YOUR POWERS AND TRUST!

SO WE WOULD'VE BECOME GUARDIANS ANYWAY, JUST ONE DAY LATER.

WE CAN LOOK AT AS MANY ALTERNATE PASTS AS YOU LIKE, BUT NOTHING WOULD CHANGE.

WHY, ORACLE? YOU SAID THAT CHANGE IS THE NATURE OF THINGS.

WELL, WILL, THIS IS THE EXCEPTION TO THE RULE!

YOU ARE THE *CHOSEN ONES*, AND YOUR PAST IS DETERMINED BY A SPECIAL, EXTRAORDINARY FORCE!

DESTINY!

SOMETHING THAT CAN DEFY EVEN THE MOST IMPENETRABLE MYSTERY OF THE UNIVERSE—

IT'S NOT ALL GONE, THOUGH. WE STILL HAVE OUR **ETERNAL** GIFTS!*

*A KIND OF **MAGICAL SUBSTANCE** THAT REMAINS DORMANT INSIDE GUARDIANS EVEN AFTER LEAVING THEIR ROLES.

EXACTLY! I HAVE A PRIVILEGED RELATIONSHIP WITH AQUATIC CREATURES.

BUT THAT'S NOT WHY YOU DECIDED TO BECOME A VETERINARIAN.

IT WAS BECAUSE OF THAT BLOND GUY YOU DUMPED...WHAT WAS HIS NAME?

YOU DO REALIZE YOU'RE HILARIOUS? YOU SHOULD'VE BECOME A STAND-UP COMEDIAN, NOT A PSYCHOL-OGIST!

BY THE WAY, HOW'S YOUR THESIS ABOUT **CONFLICT MANAGEMENT** GOING?

GOOD! APART FROM THE FACT THAT I'M THE FIRST TO GET **FIRED UP** OVER NOTHING!

THE TRUTH IS, MY **SUPERVISOR** IS USELESS.

LEMME GUESS, YOUR ETERNAL GIFT ISN'T PATIENCE!

YEAH, I NEVER FEEL COLD. NOT SO USEFUL...APART FROM THE FACT THAT I NEVER NEED HEAVY CLOTHES!

YOUR PARENTS AREN'T GIVING UP... THEY KEEP BUYING YOU SWEATERS!

WILL! YOU KNOW MS. RUDOLPH NEVER **LEGALLY** MADE THIS HOUSE OURS.

BUT IT'S LIKE SHE DID!

IF ONLY ORUBE HADN'T GONE BACK TO BASILIADE...

IT HAPPENED A LONG TIME AGO. WITHOUT KANDRAKAR'S MAGICAL SUPPORT...

...IT WAS INEVITABLE SOMEONE WOULD TAKE AN INTEREST IN THIS PROPERTY.

HAVE YOU NOTICED THAT WHEN IRMA'S AROUND, ANDREW GETS MUCH NICER?

LET US IN! I'M ASKING YOU FOR THE LAST TIME!

OH, VERY WELL. GET YOUR STUFF— BUT HURRY! I GOTTA SEND A REPORT TO THE OFFICE TOMORROW MORNING!

EITHER HE LIKES YOU, OR HE REMEMBERS THAT TIME YOU TURNED HIM INTO A TOAD!*

I-I'M SORRY! YOU'RE HERE ILLEGALLY AND...AND...

* AS SEEN IN W.I.T.C.H. CHAPTER 2

109

111

BYE!

I'M OFF! SEE YOU TOMORROW TO UNLOAD THE PICKUP.

OKAY! AND THANKS!

I'M EXHAUSTED! IF WE STILL HAD OUR POWERS...

...WE COULD'VE **TELEPORTED** EVERYTHING IN AN INSTANT!

YEAH. AND ANDREW HORNBY WOULD BE CROAKING IN A POND!

OH, IT WASN'T SO BAD! WE MANAGED.

YOU THINK WE GOT IT ALL?

OUR WHOLE PAST!

YEAH. IT'S ALL HERE, PACKED AND CATALOGED.

OH, C'MON! THAT CAN'T BE ME! I'M NOT THAT... THAT...

BORING?

NAGGY?

THE YOU IN THE HOURGLASS *COULD* BE YOU...IF YOU MAKE CERTAIN CHOICES...

YOU UGLY WITCHES! I'M NOT LIKE THAT!

YOU'RE SEEING ONE POSSIBLE FUTURE, BUT YOU COULD LIVE ANOTHER THOUSAND LIVES— ANOTHER THOUSAND FUTURES!

THANK GOODNESS. THAT ONE WAS THE PITS!

IRMA, "NORMAL" LIFE IS NOT ALWAYS FULL OF ACTION, BUT THAT DOES NOT MAKE IT ANY LESS DIFFICULT OR EXCITING.

NOW, OBSERVE. THIS JOURNEY INTO THE FUTURE IS ABOUT TO END RIGHT WHERE IT ALL *STARTED*...

"...IN HAY LIN'S KITCHEN!"

YOU, IRMA, WILL HAVE POWER OVER *ICED TEA,* UNBROKEN AND UNCONTAINABLE...

117

I JUST KNOW HE'S AN EDITOR FOR THE HEATHERFIELD TRIBUNE.

BUT BEFORE THAT, HE WORKED FOR A BIG PUBLISHER SPECIALIZING IN *FANTASY* NOVELS!

YOU MEAN HE...?

HE READ MY STUFF AND FOUND SOMETHING GOOD!

...THEN HE ASKED IF HE COULD SHOW A FRIEND, AND THIS IS THE RESULT!

A...A CHECK?

I DIDN'T WANT TO JINX IT BY SAYING ANYTHING. IT WAS HARD TO KEEP IT A SECRET!

A CHECK! AND THERE'S LOADS OF ZEROES!

ALL THAT MONEY... THAT'S...

THAT'S *OURS!* AND IT'S JUST THE ADVANCE!

OF COURSE, IF THE NOVEL BECOMES A *BESTSELLER*... AND IF THE SEQUEL THAT I'M ABOUT TO WRITE...

HEY, HANG ON A MINUTE!

119

END OF
CHAPTER 50

Out of Control

"Some people are really special,
like a comforting hug."

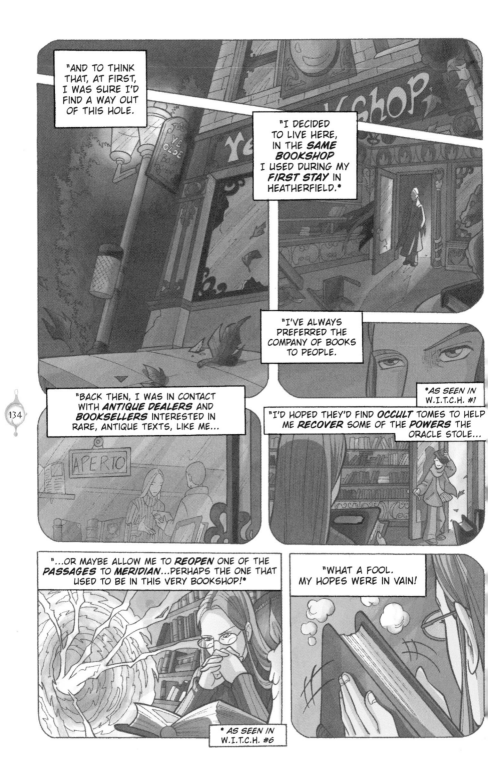

"ANGER TOWARD YOU, ORACLE, AND ESPECIALLY TOWARD...

"...THE FIVE *GUARDIANS* WHO KEPT THWARTING MY PLANS!

"EVEN IF I NEVER RETURN TO METAMOOR OR GET MY POWERS BACK, *MY TIME HERE* IN HEATHERFIELD WILL *NOT* HAVE BEEN *IN VAIN*...

136

"...BECAUSE I WILL USE *EVERY MEANS* AT MY DISPOSAL TO TURN THIS FORCED EXILE...

"...INTO MERCILESS *REVENGE* AGAINST THOSE FIVE GIRLS!"

NOW THAT I'M LIVING AMONGST THEM, I'LL HAVE TIME TO STUDY AND UNDERSTAND THEM...

...TO ANALYZE THEIR WEAKNESSES AND FEARS...

...ENABLING ME TO STRIKE THEM AT THE RIGHT MOMENT...

...CATCHING THEM COMPLETELY *UNPREPARED* AND *DEFENSELESS!*

"I JUST HAVE TO PLAY *THE ROLE* OF THE HELPFUL *ASSISTANT* TO THE STUDENTS WHO'VE BEGUN VISITING MY SHOP SINCE IT REOPENED.

"AFTER ALL, I SIMPLY HAVE TO CULTIVATE *MY TWO PASSIONS*: RARE ANTIQUE BOOKS..."

137

... AND THE *ART OF DECEIT!**

*AS SEEN IN W.I.T.C.H. CHAPTER 46

TLING

138

FOR AN INSTANT,
MATT'S AND CEDRIC'S
EYES MEET...

...RECALLING THE
TERRIBLE MOMENT
THEY FOUGHT EACH
OTHER FOR WILL
AND THE HEART OF
KANDRAKAR...*

A SINGLE,
SHARED EVENT!

*AS SEEN IN
W.I.T.C.H. CHAPTER 40

FOR CEDRIC, THAT MEMORY IS *CRYSTAL CLEAR*, AND IT UNLEASHES A WAVE OF *HATRED* TOWARD MATT...

YOUNG OLSEN! LOOKS LIKE WE'RE DESTINED TO MEET AGAIN, YOU AND I.

...HATRED HE MANAGES TO HIDE BEHIND A *MASK!*

BUT THIS TIME I WON'T LET YOU INTER-FERE!

FOR MATT, HOWEVER, THE MEMORY IS *CONFUSED* AND *MURKY*...

HUH? WHAT'S GOING ON? THAT GUY'S EYES GIVE ME THE CREEPS! I HAVE THE FEELING I'VE SEEN HIM SOMEWHERE BEFORE...

...BUT WHERE? AND WHEN?

TUMP

THE SHOCK OF THAT UNEXPECTED, FRIGHTENING EXPERIENCE CLOUDS HIS MEMORY.

HELLO, YOUNG MAN. MAY I HELP YOU?

Y-YES, THANKS...I...

IT'S A STRANGE, *SUSPENDED* INSTANT....THAT FADES TO NORMALCY...

...AS THE INEXPLICABLE, UNEASY FEELING VANISHES!

I WAS LOOKING FOR A POETRY BOOK...

ANYWAY, I WANT TO FIND OUT MORE...

ABOUT MS. KNICKERBOCHER?

OOF! ABOUT LUDMOORE!

WELL, SORRY I CAN'T HELP YOU...

...BUT I'M SURE I KNOW SOMEONE WHO'D BE *HONORED* TO HELP YOU OUT!

HELLO, GIRLS!

GOOD AFTERNOON!

HI, PROF!

Collins teaches history, and he LOVES LEGENDS.

"I'M SURE HE CAN'T WAIT TO TELL YOU *EVERYTHING HE KNOWS* ON THE SUBJECT... SINCE WE DON'T TEND TO LISTEN WHEN HE GIVES ONE OF HIS BORING LECTURES."

...AND IT WAS ON THAT OCCASION THAT THE GENERAL GAVE HIS FAMOUS SPEECH...

144

I'VE GOT SOMETHING TO TELL YOU, HAY LIN. I NEVER WANTED THIS DAY TO COME, BUT SOMETIMES YOU'RE *FORCED TO MAKE A CHOICE*, AND...WELL...

...I'VE *DECIDED TO GO* WITH MY PARENTS. WE'RE MOVING TO *OPEN HILL.**

SO FOR THE FIRST TIME SINCE I WAS LITTLE, WE'LL BE TOGETHER AGAIN... *A REAL FAMILY!*

**AS SEEN IN CHAPTER 49*

IT WASN'T AN EASY CHOICE, BUT...

...I THINK IT'S THE RIGHT ONE.

I THINK SO TOO.

155

SOME DAYS ARE SO *DARK*, YOU HAVE TO PUT THE LIGHTS ON EARLY IN THE MORNING.

DAYS WHEN THE SKY IS GLOOMY AND THREATENING RAIN...AND YOU CAN ALMOST FEEL THE *STORM BREWING* INSIDE.

DARK DAYS THAT MAKE EVERYTHING SEEM INSIGNIFICANT.

DAYS THAT LEAVE YOU *SPEECHLESS*, FOR WHATEVER REASON.

TODAY IS ONE OF THOSE DAYS. A DAY *WITHOUT* ANSWERS.

TA RA TA

159

OUCH! LOOKS PAINFUL!

YES, BUT IT DIDN'T HELP MUCH...

IT STILL LOOKS SWOLLEN! DID YOU DISINFECT IT?

IT'S STILL *BURNING!*

LET ME TAKE A LOOK.

NO WORRIES. IT'S ONLY A SCRATCH.

O-OOOH! *DR. HALE* MADE HER DIAGNOSIS!

EVER THOUGHT OF GOING TO MED SCHOOL, CORNY? I CAN TOTALLY SEE YOU PARADING AROUND THE HOSPITAL IN GREEN SCRUBS!

IRMA!

167

What's she doing?

I dunno!

HUH?

SHUSH!

As soon as she touched Taranee's scratch, Cornelia shivered, then she closed her eyes and...

ARE YOU OKAY? WHAT HAPPENED?

UNBELIEVABLE!

IT'S BETTER! I DUNNO HOW...BUT SHE DID IT!

I FELT A *WARMTH* ON MY WRIST, THEN...THE BURNING STARTED FADING...

IT WAS THE *WARMTH OF THE EARTH!*

THE SAME WARMTH THAT'S BEEN ENABLING ME TO REVIVE DEAD PLANTS AND FLOWERS...

169

"...AND CREATE CRACKS IN THE GROUND AND CLOSE THEM BACK UP."

KWIIIN

I'VE OFTEN DONE STUFF LIKE THAT, BUT I DIDN'T THINK IT WOULD WORK ON PEOPLE TOO!

WHAT'D I TELL YA? YOU'D MAKE A GREAT DOCTOR!

IN THE END, DID HE MANAGE TO DOMINATE THE FIVE ELEMENTS?

WHAT HAPPENED TO THE BOOK?

WERE THERE MORE SIGHTINGS OF THOSE...MONSTERS?

COMPLETELY OUT OF THE BLUE, LUDMOORE DISAPPEARED. NOBODY EVER SAW HIM AGAIN.

MAYBE HE FELT THAT THE SUSPICIONS AND HOSTILITY OF THE PEOPLE OF HEATHERFIELD WERE TOO MUCH FOR HIM TO WORK IN PEACE...AND HE SLUNK OFF. LUDMOORE MANOR FELL INTO DISREPAIR. IT WAS ALREADY IN A BAD STATE BECAUSE ITS TENANT...

...NEVER ALLOWED STRANGERS INTO THE HOUSE, INCLUDING SERVANTS WHO COULD'VE TAKEN CARE OF SUCH A HUGE BUILDING.

AFTER LUDMOORE DISAPPEARED, NOBODY WANTED TO LIVE IN THAT SINISTER PLACE. RUMOR HELD IT WAS STILL *INFESTED* BY HIS PRESENCE.

THE VILLA STILL EXISTS OUTSIDE HEATHERFIELD, BUT IT'LL BE DEMOLISHED SOON. THE GRAND-SON OF THE OLD OWNERS WANTS TO BUILD SOMETHING ELSE ON THE LAND.

181

UM...APART FROM LUDMOORE...YOU MENTIONED THE FIVE ELEMENTS?

YES... BUT, YOU KNOW... JUST LEGENDS. I WOULDN'T KNOW WHAT THE ELEMENTS REPRESENT...

I THINK I DO...

ME TOO...I THINK IT HAS SOMETHING TO DO WITH US!

SO, MR. COLLINS, IF THIS STORY WERE TRUE, IT WOULD PROVE THAT OURS IS, IN A WAY, A *MAGICAL CITY!*

AND THAT MAYBE THE PRESENCE OF *W.I.T.C.H.* IN HEATHERFIELD IS NO *ACCIDENT!*

WELL, WHAT DO THEY SAY? EVERY LEGEND HAS SOME TRUTH TO IT!

ANYWAY, I'D RATHER BELIEVE IN *ANOTHER KIND OF MAGIC!*

SO DID MY *WIZARD BEWITCH* HIS AUDIENCE?

UM... I THINK IT'S YOUR COOKIES THAT ARE *BEWITCHING!*

END OF
CHAPTER 51

The Book's Eye

"Beautiful and melancholic. It reminds me of the garden of the Murmurers in Meridian..."

BEAUTIFUL AND MELANCHOLIC... IT REMINDS ME OF THE GARDEN OF THE MURMURERS IN MERIDIAN...*

*CHAPTER 4

THE PLACE WHERE I HOPED *PHOBOS* WOULD WELCOME ME.

SO MANY VAIN HOPES! SO MANY BROKEN DREAMS! ALL BECAUSE OF *W.I.T.C.H.*!

IT'S THEIR FAULT I FIND MYSELF TRAPPED IN A *WORLD* I HATE.

GRUNCH

PANT!

CEDRIC IS PLAGUED WITH SIGHS, BUT TODAY, HE ISN'T ALONE...

WHOSE, LOUISE? IF IT'S ONE OF MINE, I'M NOT HOME!

HILARIOUS. IT'S HAY LIN!

HI! COME WITH ME. ERIC'S INSIDE!

UM...THANKS, MRS. LYNDON! I SEE YOU'RE ALL PACKED...

YES, WE'RE LEAVING SOON! I'M GLAD YOU CAME. I'M ALWAYS HAPPY TO SEE YOU!

SHE'S *LYING.* I CAN *FEEL* IT! THE TRUTH IS SHE THINKS I'M WEIRD...AND IT'S MY FAULT!

THE FIRST TIME WE MET, I SPILLED SOUP ON HER. THE SECOND, I ALMOST BROKE THAT THING...*

*CHAPTERS 44 AND 45

"...THE ASTROLABE!"

BE CAREFUL HOW YOU PACK IT!

206

BUT MY VISIONS HAVE TO BE INTERPRETED IN SOME WAY!

OKAY, BUT WHAT'S SO CREEPY ABOUT AN EYE WITH A GUITAR?

MAYBE IT SEEMS WEIRD BECAUSE IT PLAYS...*BY EAR!* HEE-HEE!

WHEN I GET THE JOKE, I'LL LET YOU KNOW...

OKAY, GUYS, THAT'S ENOUGH. WHATEVER IRMA'S VISIONS MAY MEAN...

"...ALL THAT MATTERS IS THAT MATT'S ALL RIGHT!"

SORRY... HERE. I'VE SWITCHED OFF MY PHONE.

THAT'S BETTER, BOY.

THAT'S MUCH BETTER!

219

OTHER DOUBTS, ANOTHER SCENARIO. AT YE OLDE BOOKSHOP.

WE'RE CLOSED!

I KNOW WE'RE USUALLY OPEN ON SUNDAY MORNING, BUT WE GOT SOME NEW BOOKS AND ARE CLOSED...

...FOR INVENTORY.

HMM...GOOD. I WISH I COULD SAY I'M GLAD TO SEE YOU, MISS REBECCA... WHAT WAS IT? RUDOLPH?

ORUBE.

ORUBE! OF COURSE. AFTER ALL, I HAVE NO CUSTOMERS TODAY...

HIS EYES...

HOW DID YOU GET BACK IN? I DIDN'T HEAR THE BELL...

I'M GOOD AT MOVING QUIETLY WHEN I WANT TO.

AND WHAT IS THAT SUPPOSED TO BE?

TAKE-OUT ITALIAN-STYLE CAPPUCCINO—A REAL TREAT!

IT'S FROM THE BAR NEXT DOOR. EVER BEEN THERE?

NO. I'M NOT INTERESTED IN EXPLORING THE AREA...

...OR THE CITY OR THE WHOLE PLANET, FOR THAT MATTER.

YOU TALK AS IF YOU WERE JUST PASSING THROUGH.

WHAT IS IT YOU WANT?

TASTE IT. I DISCOVERED IT A WHILE AGO WHILE WALKING AROUND HEATHERFIELD...

...WONDERING WHAT I WAS DOING IN THIS PART OF THE WORLD.

AHEM!

ALL RIGHT, I'LL REPHRASE THE QUESTION. WHAT WOULD YOU LIKE?

SOME OLD BOOKS!

MORE RESEARCH FOR YOUR MAGAZINE?

NO. I'M JUST CURIOUS.

THE LAST TIME I WAS HERE, I READ SOME TEXTS ABOUT SOMEONE WHO LIVED IN HEATHERFIELD MANY YEARS AGO...

...A CERTAIN *LUDMOORE!*

I SEE...BUT THE BOOK-SHOP IS IN DISARRAY. YOU PROBABLY WON'T FIND THOSE BOOKS ON THE SAME SHELVES.

THIS ISN'T THE PLACE FOR THAT STUFF. BESIDES, THIS IS IMPORTANT TOO...

...I GOTTA FIND OUT WHAT MATT WOULD LIKE FOR OUR *ANNIVER-SARY*...

A *LIFE-AND-DEATH* ISSUE!

THEY'RE SPLITTING UP! TARANEE, HURRY!

LET'S GO, WILL! AT LEAST I'LL BE AWAY FROM CORNELIA.

OH NO! PETER'S LEAFING THROUGH AN OLD ICE SKATING MAGAZINE.

SO?

THERE'S A *PICTURE* OF ME IN IT THAT THEY TOOK WHEN I WON REGIONALS.

235

I HAVE TO DESTROY IT! I LOOK *AWFUL* IN THAT PICTURE!

STOP! WHAT ARE YOU DOING?

OLD MAGAZINE

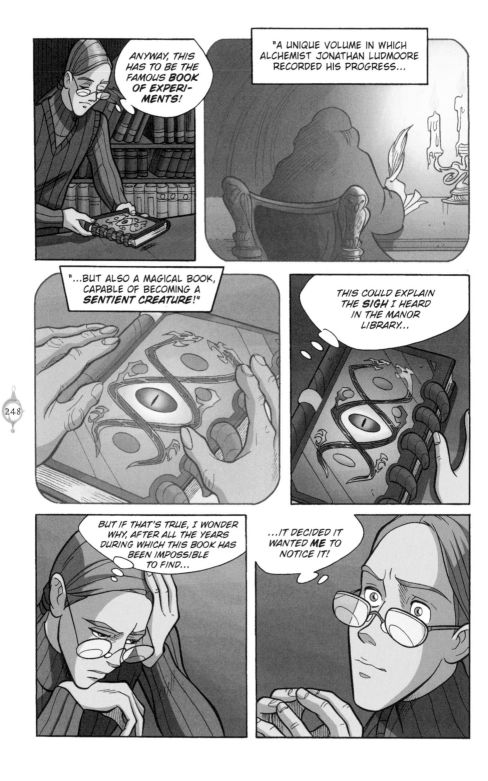

SPACK

?

TH-THE LIGHT! IT WENT OUT!

WHEN IT DID, I THOUGHT I HEARD SOMETHING—LIKE A NOISE...

...OR EVEN A SENTENCE IN THE DIALECT OF **METAMOOR!**

COME ON, CEDRIC! I KNOW YOU MISS HOME, BUT THIS IS RIDICUL—

249

*I'M PLEASED TO MEET YOU.

Read on in Volume 14!

Discover the room of...

Explore
Matt's Room

He loves music, sports, and much more.
Let's explore Matt's room to discover his secrets.

- Reserved and pretty **shy** with girls, Matt tends to blush a lot. He's the guitarist of **Cobalt Blue**, Sheffield Institute's most popular band.

- You can find him at the **pet shop** that belongs to his grandpa, Mr. Olsen, where he "pretends" to help out, or at home with a friend (usually Joel) **playing guitar** and listening to music. He plays basketball with Peter: They're on the same team.

- He's a bit lazy and loves spending the afternoon browsing Heatherfield's **music shops** looking for rare CDs.

- He's in love with **Will**, and it was hard for him to find the courage to declare his feelings. Their relationship is at a crossroads! Read the story to find out what happened.

- Matt is a senior at Heatherfield High School. His zodiac sign is **Leo**.

- Some mornings he looks in the mirror and is pleased with his look. Other days, he'd like to empty his wardrobe, join the gym, and become like **his cousin Sean**.

- He'd love to travel the world, and his **dream** is to become a musician.

Discover Matt's Room

Matt loves sci-fi novels.

When he's sad or wants to relax, Matt plays guitar and pictures himself in front of a cheering audience.

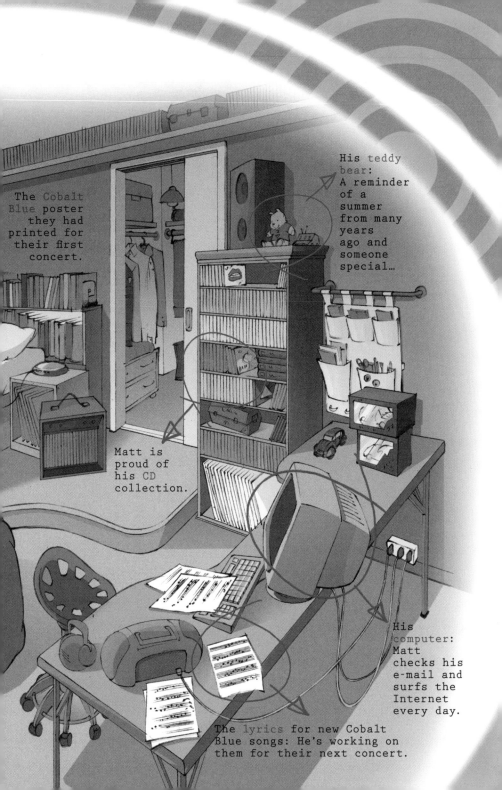

Part V: The Book of Elements • Volume 1

Series Created by Elisabetta Gnone
Comic Art Direction: Alessandro Barbucci, Barbara Canepa

W.I.T.C.H.: The Graphic Novel, Part V: The Book of Elements © Disney Enterprises, Inc.

English translation © 2019 by Disney Enterprises, Inc.

Yen Press, LLC supports the right to free expression and the value of copyright. The purpose of copyright is to encourage writers and artists to produce the creative works that enrich our culture.

The scanning, uploading, and distribution of this book without permission is a theft of the author's intellectual property. If you would like permission to use material from the book (other than for review purposes), please contact the publisher. Thank you for your support of the author's rights.

JY
1290 Avenue of the Americas
New York, NY 10104

Visit us at jyforkids.com
facebook.com/jyforkids
twitter.com/jyforkids
jyforkids.tumblr.com
instagram.com/jyforkids

First JY Edition: January 2019

JY is an imprint of Yen Press, LLC.
The JY name and logo are trademarks of Yen Press, LLC.

The publisher is not responsible for websites (or their content) that are not owned by the publisher.

Library of Congress Control Number: 2017950917

ISBNs:
978-1-9753-8377-0 (paperback)
978-1-9753-8378-7 (ebook)

10 9 8 7 6 5 4 3 2 1

LSC-C

Printed in the United States of America

Cover Art by Manuela Razzi
Colors by Andrea Cagol

Translation by Linda Ghio and Stephanie Dagg at Editing Zone
Lettering by Katie Blakeslee

BETWEEN DREAM AND REALITY

Concept and Script by Teresa Radice
Layout and pencils by Alberto Zanon
Inks by Riccardo Sisti
Color and Light Direction by Francesco Legramandi
Title Page Art by Alberto Zanon with colors by Andrea Cagol

IT'S MAGICAL ANYWAY

Concept and Script by Bruno Enna
Layout by Daniela Vetro
Pencils by Federico Bertolucci
Inks by Marina Baggio
Color and Light Direction by Francesco Legramandi
Title Page Art by Giada Perissinotto
with colors by Andrea Cagol

OUT OF CONTROL

Concept and Script by Teresa Radice
Layout and Pencils by Giada Perissinotto
Inks by Marina Baggio and Roberta Zanotta
Color and Light Direction by Francesco Legramandi
Title Page Art by Giada Perissinotto
with colors by Andrea Cagol

THE BOOK'S EYE

Concept and Script by Bruno Enna
Layout and Pencils by Federico Bertolucci, Flavia Scuderi, and Monica Catalano
Inks by Marina Baggio and Santa Zangari
Color and Light Direction by Francesco Legramandi
Title Page Art by Giada Perissinotto
with colors by Andrea Cagol